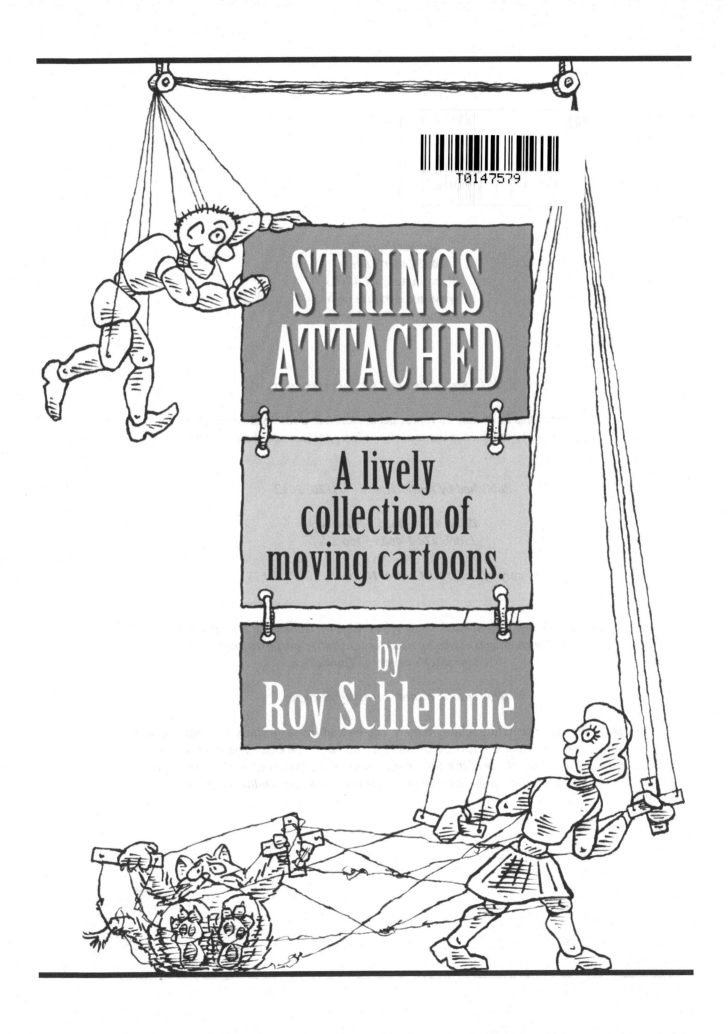

AuthorHouse™
1663 Liberty Drive
Bloomington, IN 47403
www.authorhouse.com
Phone: 1-800-839-8640

Published by AuthorHouse   03/20/2012

ISBN: 978-1-4685-5467-0 (sc)
ISBN: 978-1-4685-5466-3 (e)

Library of Congress Control Number: 2012903133

Any people depicted in stock imagery provided by Thinkstock are models, and such images are being used for illustrative purposes only. Certain stock imagery © Thinkstock.

This book is printed on acid-free paper.

Because of the dynamic nature of the Internet, any web addresses or links contained in this book may have changed since publication and may no longer be valid. The views expressed in this work are solely those of the author and do not necessarily reflect the views of the publisher, and the publisher hereby disclaims any responsibility for them.

For TC and Nancy,
The Chelsea Cosmopolites.

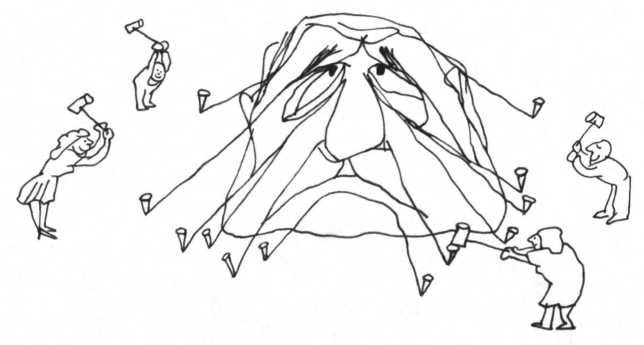

No laugh lines here!

However, you might find a few augmenting
some of my little cartoon efforts contained on
the next 126 pages. If you're partial to
boisterous, exuberant, and rambunctious
humor, then you've come to the right place
for a bit of light-hearted entertainment.
Although nobody's offering anything like
a money-back guarantee here, I do feel
that, even if, like the beleagured soul
seen above, you're bummed out by more
than a few of life's pervasive little problems,
my upbeat collection of oddball gems
should provide a welcome respite.

—Roy Schlemme

R. SCHLEMME

BRANCUSI
ROMANIAN
(1879-1929)

OLDENBERG
AMERICAN
(1929-   )

LOPEZ
CUSTODIAN
(1973-   )

R.SCHLEMME

"Were it my duel, sir, I'd be
focusing on his oxygen bottle."

"Perhaps, if you stopped feeding them flies,
they <u>would</u> all go away."

"Never let it be said that management doesn't listen... Here's your raise in celery."

"Still windy out there?"

"Even though I'm no art critic,
I'd have to rate this as probably
his most noteworthy creative effort."

"Compliments of the exterminator at Table Twelve."

"We use them for emergencies whenever
Economy Class video goes down."

"It never comes out quite as well
with reconstituted eye of newt."

"Stop delivering motivational lectures to
that pile of stones. Our kids are over here."

"Damn, that *Titanic* bunch sure knows
how to throw all-night parties!"

"If it seems a bit snug, you may
want to try this one instead."

"My writing success is a result of clever plot development, an encyclopedic knowledge of language and a publishing house run by shamelessly biased, pushy relatives."

"If it says there are worms here,
then there must be worms here."

"So, by how much do you think these
racing stripes might boost your speed?"

"No, thanks. I'm pretty well stuffed already."

"Look, the kid hit .310 in Triple A with that stance, so I wouldn't tamper."

"How's this baby handle in swill?"

"Please don't leave, Helen...
I can change!"

"It doesn't promote hair growth, but it will
shrink your head about two sizes."

"Besides enhancing my home entertainment value,
'Tap' also gets me occasional small club dates."

A Wonder Drug.

"With minimal chair realignment here,
we could play *Choo-choo Train*."

"Any problem with me
taking off this afternoon?"

"This is the last time we do
theater before antler-shedding season."

R.SCHLEMME

"Am I headed right for
the Salzburg Music Festival?"

R. SCHLEMME

"Pecs Patrol...eyes right!"

"Is this what you meant about *'becoming one with nature'*?"

"I'm sensing an imminent draw due to cobwebs."

"For a modest fee, I could redo
these little babies in anthracite."

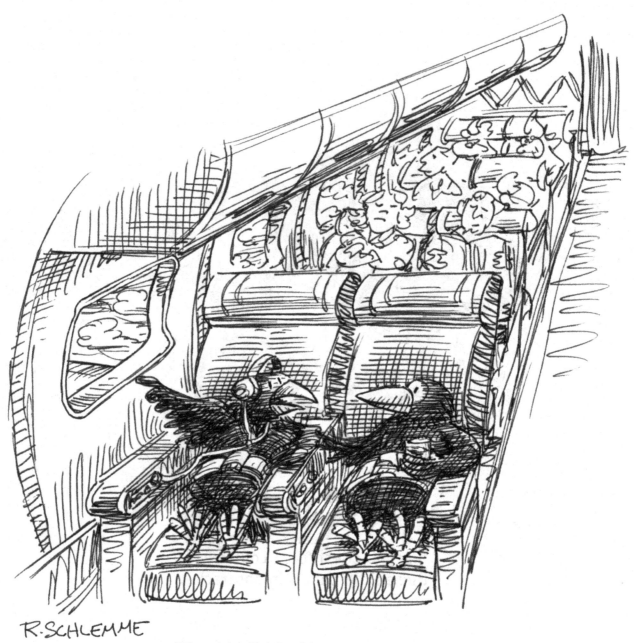

R·SCHLEMME

"Frankly, I'd feel lots more secure
seeing feathers on those wings."

"...and over to the right of *Carlo the Snitch* just beyond
Denny the Narc, you've got *Linda the Parole Officer*."

"One would hope that, after ten years in the service, you'd have mastered 'The Tunic Buttoning Thing'."

R. SCHLEMME

"You couldn't pay me enough
to dress in primary colors."

R. SCHLEMME

PET GUILT TRIPS

R. SCHLEMME

"Hopefully, one day I'll be treated
better by your great-grandchildren."

An offering in the Cathedral of Nature.

"So you really feel that someday
it could replace the broadsword?"

"I'd like to run a few tests first."

"I give it one winter."

How traffic lights amuse themselves.

R. SCHLEMME

"Know that strike zone you've had trouble locating?
It's just turned up in Keokuk."

"Does this reclassify our annual *Pick-your-own-pumpkin Fest*
as a bygone tradition of rural America?"

"Thanks, but I never could've gotten where I am without those leadership seminars."

R. SCHLEMME

"Sir, you might find something more suitable over in our *'Lard Ass'* chair section."

"Contact our temp agency for someone to
analyze data, collate reports and kiss my patootie."

"Is there an ocean somewhere
in the neighborhood?"

"Anybody here know how
to spell *'independence'*?"

"I'm told it really helps to shift
weight onto the balls of your feet."

"The employment agency felt your
company could use a good goose."

Had FDR given his famous speech today...

R. SCHLEMME

"Nuthin's gonna be resolved here till
somebody gits down off'n his high horse."

"...and for someone
at our table, <u>no</u> dessert."

R. SCHLEMME

"Diagrams, MacFarland! People need diagrams!"

"Pond Rule Number One: Biggest frog occupies
biggest lily pad. There is no Pond Rule Number Two."

"Good luck, Hal! If anyone's able to find
World War II up there, it's you!"

"It says, 'Curse continued on column four, upper level, queen's chamber'."

R. SCHLEMME

"What a nice day! Why don't you little guys
all go out and play in the sunshine and filth?"

R. SCHLEMME

"Honestly, there's absolutely nothing
under your bed. So go to sleep."

"It's bright...it's hot...and I like it!"

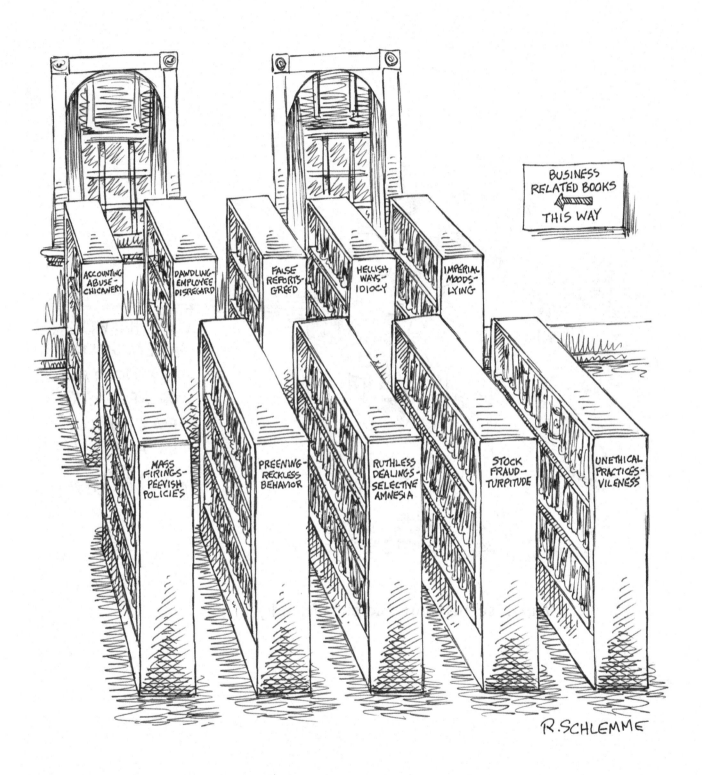

" 'Bang!' seems more audience-friendly."

"Nature often says 'Hi!' in mysterious ways."

"Duck! Flying frisbee dog!"

"Stop staring!"

R.SCHLEMME

"Have a nice day."

R. SCHLEMME

"Looks like we'll be needing an
adjective change for *Hubert the Mild*."

R. SCHLEMME

"Sure, Larry, comfort and style are big, but let's take a look at another quality that the ideal sock mask should have."

R.SCHLEMME

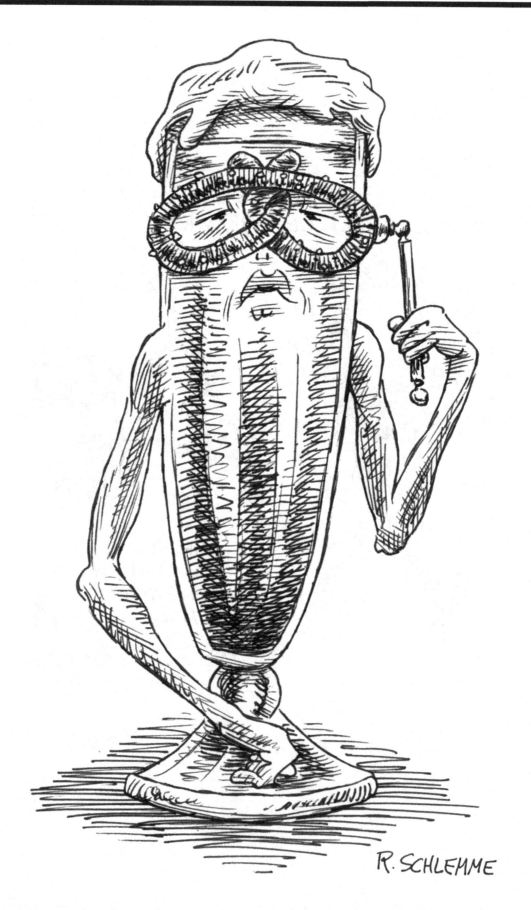

R. SCHLEMME

"You'll really be amazed at how quickly
nature sharpens the other senses
in order to compensate."

"Creativity never sleeps."

"Behold, God has chosen to send
His great message through me!"

"I find myself yet another victim of
the *'All giraffes look alike'* stereotype."

Culinary Olympics.
(10-meter mixed salad spatula diving.)

R.SCHLEMME

R. SCHLEMME

R. SCHLEMME

Theater Lobby Interrogation.

"Hi! Welcome to our *'Stuff that I've always treasured but my wife will toss once my back is turned'* Museum."

"Portion control, everyone...portion control!"

"As much as you all enjoyed it, three encores
on Schubert's *'Trout Quintet'* will have to suffice."

"Not without some ID."

"Something casual, light and able to correct a congenital lurch."

R. SCHLEMME

"Considering today's medical
advances, I see no reason why we can't
match your old raisin perfectly."

"It has twelve tuberous appendages,
a spikey variegated exoskeleton and
seems to be giving me *the Finger*."

"Frankly, the last place I'd ever pick to
recover from eating some bad fish is
a buoy that's rocking...rocking...rocking..."

"In this case, I don't feel that *'I'm tired of looking at his silly face'* constitutes reasonable grounds for divorce."

R. SCHLEMME

Prepared for imminent fame.

"So, right after lightning bug season, let's
get serious about that new wide-screen TV."

"From what I can see,
it's abstract and I don't like it."

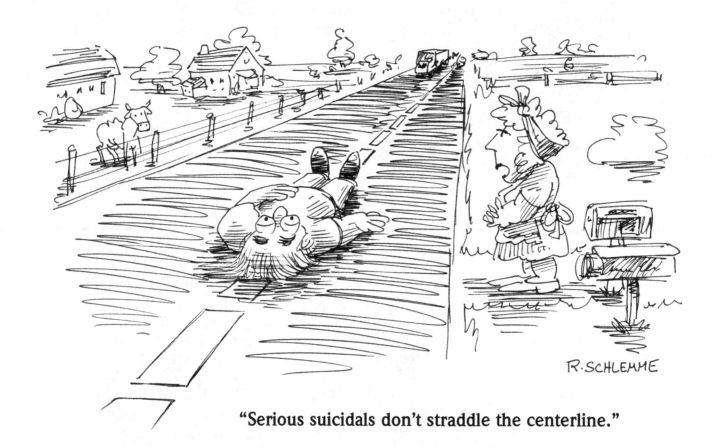

"Serious suicidals don't straddle the centerline."

"It's nice to occasionally have
one's view of the world reconfirmed."

R. SCHLEMME

"Play something *'Red, white and bluesy'*, Sam!"

"Although not enchanted, I do hold
a controlling interest in some
prime waterfront properties."

R. SCHLEMME

"The good news, kids, is...it's lunchtime!
The bad news is...we're introducing self-service!"

"I wouldn't be overly concerned. It's only a phase."

"Stupid question! Can daisies get a hernia?"

"The hell with social graces...
I want a chicken salad sandwich."

R. SCHLEMME

"And you ask, *'Why cats?'*."

R. SCHLEMME

"Let the hunting season
surprise counterattack begin."

R.SCHLEMME

"I get high on helium."

R. SCHLEMME

R. SCHLEMME

"Jensen, I'll never be able to
experience true deprivation if you
keep offering me light refreshments."

"Doug's had another rough workday.
He's down in the pool right now."

"...and in this corner, with the gray trunk and weighing 9,472 pounds..."

R. SCHLEMME

"Now there is a really strong argument
for switching to disposable coffee cups."

"Stock anything in a 34C
with feathers?"

"Unfortunately, madam, this isn't a genuine
Tiffany dragonfly lamp. Like us, it's only
a crudely drawn cartoonist's interpretation."

"Although it's quite good stylistically,
I find an excessive dependence on
⟨⟨⟨⟨⟨ and ⟨⟨⟨⟨⟨!"

"Sure, becoming frogs will move us up
the food chain, but all that means is going
from appetizer to main course."

Sharing an early morning bunrise.

R. SCHLEMME

"Lose some line weight...and fast!"

"Say, here's an exciting weekend coming up!
Booked for two wedding parties...
and I'm the groom in both!"

R. SCHLEMME

LONE RANGER | ZORRO | GREEN HORNET

THE DUNKELMANNS

R. SCHLEMME

"I have a confession. I don't contain
all the nutritional supplements needed
for the growth of strong teeth and bones."

R. SCHLEMME

"Actually, I'm sort of relieved that
they don't appear overly advanced."

"Don't get picky. In this day and age, we take
our wetlands wherever we find them."

" *'Sit'*...but if you are sitting...*'Stand'*."

"...and why are you looking to leave
the field you're currently in?"

R. SCHLEMME

R. SCHLEMME

"Lights...camera...inaction!"

Hopefully, having finished *Strings Attached*, you're
feeling a bit more uptempo than our sedentary
gastropod in the director's chair. Dare we assume
that you might've enjoyed Schlemme's cartoon
takes to the degree that there's a desire
to view even more in the future? Well,
then, by all means, immediately contact
authorhouse.com to order one or more
of his equally entertaining offerings:
*Skewed Views, Skewed Views Too,
The Moon's First Banana, Lightin' Up*
and/or *Pull In Case Of Boredom.*